GW01086546

Special thanks to

This book has been a labour of love for our team; but there are so many who deserve our thanks for their support not just for the production of this book but also for their support of the Grainger Market Delivery project.

The Grainger Market Traders, Newcastle City Council, with a special nod to Jane Rose. Our friends at Newcastle Chronicle particularly Helen Dalby, The Sunshine Fund, Siobhan Sargeant, Lauren Thompson, the Grainger Market Delivery Team including Darren-Pierre Phillips, Emma Claude Blair Phillips & John Phillips, Sarah Anderson, Kevin Taylor, John Bonner. Also Alison Demidova, Marc-Olivier Hounsou and the Niltoni Team. Newcastle NE1 for all their support through the height of the pandemic. Our friends Amy Bunting and Helen McCabe, Jo Leversuch, Oliver William Smith, Chris Davis, Chloe Fitzpatrick, Jason Caddy, El Fegan, Daniel Wilson, Kieron Boston, Graeme Donaldson for their never ending support. Our parents Moya Scott, Gladys Clark and lastly our actors Kim Woodburn, Harper Pinnock Palmer, Harris Phillips and Noa Blair Phillips.

First Edition published 2021

This book belongs to:

_____

_____

_____

As a North East charity, supporting local children living with disabilities, additional needs and terminal illnesses, we know only too well how important it is to support local. We rely solely on the kindness and generosity of local organisations, communities and individuals to fund life-changing, specialist equipment for our children and their families.

The equipment we fund is individual to each child and their personal needs, providing them with comfort and safety, allowing them to gain independence and confidence, enabling them to learn, play and grow, giving them the opportunities they deserve to live life their way.

We wholeheartedly thank you for supporting us through buying this book which will allow us to continue to support children in need in our local communities.

From the team, families and children at The Chronicle Sunshine Fund, we wish you wonderful Christmas and New Year.

Siobhan Sargeant,
Charity Director of The Chronicle Sunshine Fund

Chronicle
SunshineFund
...changing the lives of children with disabilities

The elf who saved Christmas
was a story indeed.

We were so busy, and Christmas day
mouths to feed;

It's a story of persistence,
courage and a busy,
busy,
business!

So here's the tale of Tip Top,
the elf who saved
Christmas!

Now t'was noon on the night before, **the night before Christmas.**

Lots was stirring at Santa's workshop **and house.**

Mrs Claus was a tizzy because of **the stress,**

She wished she had **more time** instead of less!

To gather the
**presents, treats
turkey and mince pies!**

And all the important things for everyone's **festive supplies.**

Tip Top the elf was **summoned** to her kitchen table, where she gave him a list, and asked if **he was able.**

To head to the **Grainger,** a market in **'Toon'.**

Tip Top was **dizzy** with the **grand request,** But nodded his head and said **'I'll do my best!';**

...he headed for the market where he'd shop,
no hither and thither!

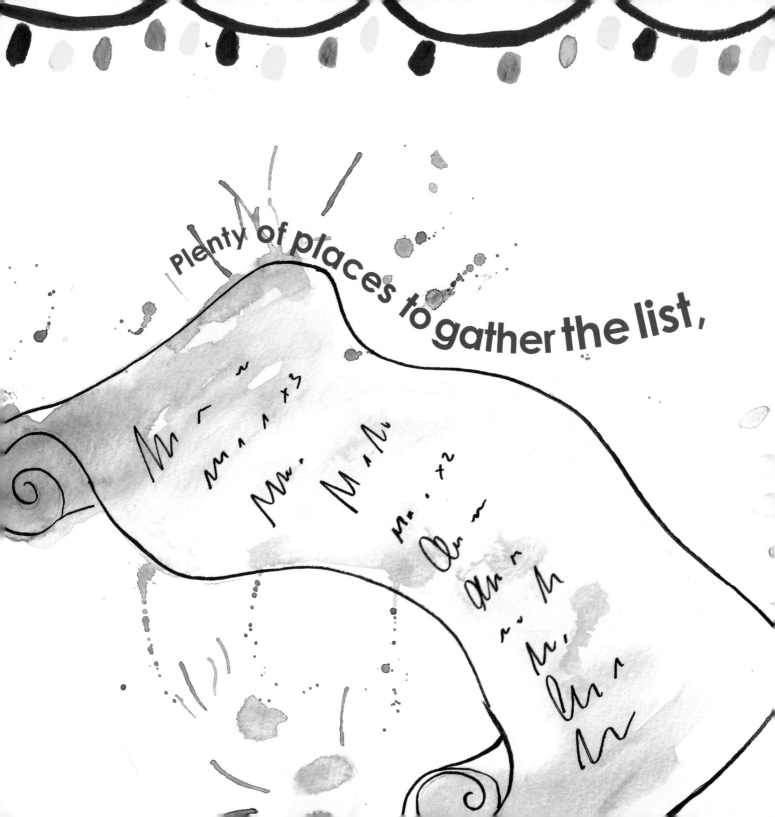

Plenty of places to gather the list,

a turkey,

a ham,

or lobster and prawns

from cold waters fished.

Sprouts,

cabbage,

carrots,

cheeses,

crackers, biscuits,

beers and wines.

'Devils on horseback' for roasting in lines.

Hampers for gifting, cards for the posting,

and plenty more treats
to share,
wether you're visiting
or hosting.

Calamity struck!

Just when Tip Top headed out!

The weather was howling a hideous

shout!

It heralded rain,

sleet
then
heavy snow,

but Tip Top headed onward, to the market he must go!

Struggle he did through the

blizzards

and

worse!

Under his breath he whispered a curse...

For how would Tip Top
get to the market in time?
The bus was full, and the taxis had a long line.

Through the snow a cafe Tip Top did spy,

a hot drink of **cocoa** and a **snug** he might try.

Inside the cafe, our Elf **got a shock!**

For computers were
sat all around, so online
he would shop!

His deadline from Mrs Claus **wouldn't be missed!**

Our hero logged on Grainger Delivery, **and out came the list.**

With a **click** and a **click** he was shopping online.

No weather to battle, no taxi line!

He shopped for the gifts, wine

and beer by the barrel!

Cakes, **pies**

and sweets,

as he hummed a Christmas carol.

Saving the day he smiled inside!

Mrs Claus would be happy and he smiled with pride.

NET Cafe

"So that was Tip Top and he **saved the day!**" Mrs Claus told the crowd.

Assembled
the elves,
to who she told out loud.

Tip Top a treasure
and made
Christmas
supreme.

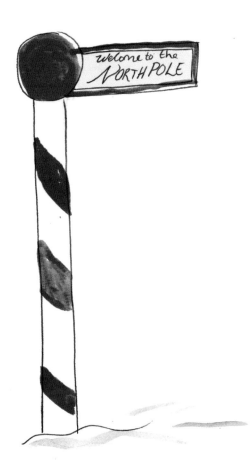

We support our local businesses
in Grainger Market.

Shop local, visit
www.graingerdelivery.com

Printed in Great Britain
by Amazon